for Nina Salkovskis
with lots of love

First U.S. edition
Text and illustrations copyright © 1995 by Debi Gliori
Copyright © 1995 by Frances Lincoln Limited

Macmillan Books for Young Readers
An imprint of Simon & Schuster Children's Publishing Division
Simon & Schuster Macmillan
1230 Avenue of the Americas
New York, New York 10020

First published in Great Britain in 1995 with the title
Little Bear and the Wish Fish, by Frances Lincoln Limited,
4 Torriano Mews, Torriano Avenue, London NW5 2RZ

Printed and bound in Hong Kong
10 9 8 7 6 5 4 3 2 1

Library of Congress Catalog Card Number: 94-078656
ISBN 0-02-736021-0

Willie Bear and the Wish Fish

DEBI GLIORI

Macmillan Books for Young Readers ● New York

Life was peachy for the Bears of Papana River Valley. They had a view of the river from their cave. The sky was dotted with gulls, the trees were laced with songbirds, and the fields were carpeted with pheasants. They fished when it rained, hunted when it snowed, and sunbathed when it was sunny.

Yet the weather was never quite right for the Bears.
They complained when it rained, "It's too wet!"
They complained when it snowed, "It's too cold!"
They even complained "It's too hot!" when the sun came out.

The weather makers were not amused.
So Rain Dancer, Snow Shaker, and Sun Blazer
decided to teach the Bears a lesson they would
never forget.

First they caught a fish.
Next they gave it the power
to grant wishes.

Then they returned the fish,
slippety slithery, to the river.

When the Bears woke up the next morning, the fog was so thick that they couldn't see anything at all.

"Wow!" said Willie Bear.

"Where are you, dear?" called Mama Bear. "You need to wear your rain suit with five zippers, if you're going out."

"This fog is awful," grumbled Papa Bear. "I wish it would snow."

All of a sudden, a blizzard bombarded the valley.
The sky turned a frosty gray. A freezing wind
turned the river into ragged, jagged icebergs.
The wish fish hid in a sheltered shallow.

"Wow!" said Willie Bear.

"Oh dear," fussed Mama Bear. "Now you need
to put on your snowsuit with forty snaps, if you're
going out."

"This snow is horrible," muttered Papa Bear.
"I wish it would be sunny."

Immediately, the snow melted and the grass singed to a crunchy brown. The river dried up to a trickle, and the wish fish flipped and flopped in a muddy puddle outside the Bears' cave as birds fainted from the heat. "Wow!" shouted Willie Bear.

"I'm so hot!
I wish I didn't
have all this fur,"
moaned Papa Bear.

Oh no!

"And I'm so sticky," groaned Mama Bear. "I wish we lived in the Arctic Ocean!"

Oh glub!

"I wish you two would stop complaining and leave me alone," said Willie Bear crossly.

Oh help!

And Willie Bear was all alone.

Willie Bear was miserable.
"I'm cold and wet and lonely," he moaned.
"I wish . . . "

Suddenly, the wish fish popped up next to him.
    "Listen, kid," it said. "Get it right this time.
One last wish—and that's it!"

Willie Bear thought hard. Waves kept slapping his muzzle and he almost wished for a cozy scarf. But he didn't.

Then the cold turned his head into a furry Popsicle and he almost wished for a woolly hat. But he didn't.

Soon Willie Bear began to sink and he *almost* wished for a life jacket. But he didn't.

Instead, he wished for the best wish of all.

"I wish I lived in a cave by a river,
with Papa Bear and Mama Bear,

and weather that snows sometimes,
rains occasionally,
and is sunny more often than not."

And . . . whoosh!

And so the Bears of Papana River Valley
returned to their charmed life.
Papa Bear's fur grew back,
Mama Bear decided that the Arctic
was no place for cave bears, and Willie Bear
taught them both to never, ever complain.

After all, life was peachy.